ONE
LAST
WORD

WISDOM FROM THE
HARLEM RENAISSANCE

Also by Nikki Grimes

Planet Middle School

ONE

LAST

WORD

WISDOM FROM THE
HARLEM RENAISSANCE

NIKKI GRIMES

ARTWORK BY

Cozbi A. Cabrera • R. Gregory Christie • Pat Cummings
Jan Spivey Gilchrist • Ebony Glenn • Nikki Grimes • E. B. Lewis
Frank Morrison • Christopher Myers • Brian Pinkney • Sean Qualls
James Ransome • Javaka Steptoe • Shadra Strickland • Elizabeth Zunon

BLOOMSBURY
NEW YORK   LONDON   OXFORD   NEW DELHI   SYDNEY

First published in the United States of America in January 2017
by Bloomsbury Children's Books
www.bloomsbury.com

Bloomsbury is a registered trademark of Bloomsbury Publishing Plc

For information about permission to reproduce selections from this book, write to Permissions, Bloomsbury Children's Books, 1385 Broadway, New York, New York 10018 Bloomsbury books may be purchased for business or promotional use. For information on bulk purchases please contact Macmillan Corporate and Premium Sales Department at specialmarkets@macmillan.com

Library of Congress Cataloging-in-Publication Data
Names: Grimes, Nikki, author. | Cabrera, Cozbi A., illustrator.
Title: One last word : wisdom from the Harlem Renaissance / Nikki Grimes ;
Illustrated by Cozbi Cabrera [and 12 others].
Description: New York : Bloomsbury USA Children's, 2017.
Identifiers: LCCN 2016016215 (print) | LCCN 2016035859 (e-book)
ISBN 978-1-61963-554-8 (hardcover) | ISBN 978-1-61963-555-5 (e-book)
Subjects: LCSH: African Americans—Poetry. | BISAC: JUVENILE NONFICTION / People & Places / United States / African American. | JUVENILE NONFICTION / History / United States / 20th Century. | JUVENILE FICTION / Stories in Verse.
Classification: LCC PS3557.R489982 A6 2017 (print) | LCC PS3557.R489982 (e-book) | DDC 811/.54—dc23
LC record available at https://lccn.loc.gov/2016016215

Book design by Jessie Gang
Printed in China by Leo Paper Products, Heshan, Guangdong
2 4 6 8 10 9 7 5 3 1

For Julius Lester, who, when I was a teen, told me that my words mattered. And I believed him.

TABLE OF CONTENTS

PART III—TO A DARK GIRL

RESOURCES

PREFACE

I was thirteen years old when I read my poetry aloud in front of an audience for the first time. The event took place at the Countee Cullen Library in New York City, a local branch named after one of the leading poets of the Harlem Renaissance.

A lover of poetry for most of my young life, I was well aware of the impact of Countee Cullen, Langston Hughes, Paul Laurence Dunbar, and all the other African American poets of the era. After all, I was a young poet born in the very Harlem from which many of their careers were launched. As I ascended the stage that day, I felt as if I were stepping into the stream of the Renaissance poets who had come before me. I feel their weight, and their influence, still. The elegance and power of their poetry gave me wings.

At the beginning of my career, my focus was on prose and poetry for the adult market. Reading my work at college campuses, I often shared the stage with the likes of Nikki Giovanni, Sonia Sanchez, and Amiri Baraka. Ultimately, though, I switched my emphasis to literature for children and young adults. Nonetheless, the poets of the Harlem Renaissance remained my primary influences.

Now that I am at a point in my career when my work is being taught in schools across the country, I want to take a moment to celebrate those earlier poets, add my voice to theirs in a very direct way, and introduce them to a new generation.

THE HARLEM RENAISSANCE

The Harlem Renaissance was one of the most remarkable periods of artistic growth and exploration in American history. This era followed the Great Migration, when millions of African Americans left the South in search of a better life. Many of them settled in Harlem, where they finally felt free to express themselves and speak their minds without fear, and one of the ways they did so was through the arts. These were the heady days of such luminaries as James Weldon Johnson, Josephine Baker, and artist Aaron Douglas. Wow!

Between 1918 and the mid- to late 1930s, an explosion of African American music, art, and literature spread from one big city to another. But it was in Harlem that the greatest number, and range, of poets and writers gathered, including Arna Bontemps, Countee Cullen, Zora Neale Hurston, Georgia Douglas Johnson, Jean Toomer, and Langston Hughes. A number of extraordinary women are usually left off that roster—Gwendolyn Bennett, Clara Ann Thompson, and Anne Spencer among them. These and other emerging African American writers found a home for their artistic self-expression in black-owned magazines and literary journals like *Fire!!*; *Opportunity*: *A Journal of Negro Life*; and the *Crisis*, published by W. E. B. Du Bois, with novelist and poet Jessie Redmon Fauset as its literary editor. In fact, black-owned newspapers and journals sprung up throughout the northern states. It was there, removed from the daily constrictions of Jim Crow laws and the constant threat of violence from the Ku Klux Klan, that African Americans spread their cultural wings and began to fly.

Personal essays, fiction, and poetry reflecting racial pride began to take center stage, while the first glimpses of black life, as seen from a black perspective, came to the fore. Together with the music, dance, and visual art created by African Americans during this era, the groundbreaking literature that sprung from the Harlem Renaissance proved to America, and the world, that there was more to the minds, hearts, and souls of black folk than previously expressed.

Through the decades, this literature has reminded readers, of all races, how vital it is that we define ourselves, set our own paths, celebrate our own capabilities, and determine our own destiny, no matter what obstacles are placed in our way.

I have been honored to attend the Coretta Scott King Book Awards Breakfast on many occasions, and whenever I rise to join in the refrain of "Lift Every Voice and Sing," by James Weldon Johnson, I feel the pull of the tether that connects me to the Harlem Renaissance. The art and literature of that era still resonates today.

Why look to writers of the Harlem Renaissance for wisdom and strength in difficult times? Because these writers, so recently removed from slavery and a Jim Crow South, survived much.

They still have much to teach us regarding toughness, survival, and a positive attitude.

These literary lights, writing at a time when the lynching of black men filled the news, were more than familiar with racial profiling, racial violence, and every variety of injustice imaginable. Yet they ascended to great heights in spite of it all. Their works exude power and wisdom aplenty. They knew the importance of telling their own stories, of presenting their own images to the world. Above all, they understood how to make the most of their freedom, despite living in a nation that had not then, and has not yet, fully realized its promise of freedom and justice for all.

AUTHOR'S NOTE

"Mother to Son" is one of the best-known and best-loved poems by Langston Hughes. For years I thought the poem was titled "The Crystal Stair" because the phrase "no crystal stair," repeated twice in the poem, is one that lingers in my memory.

"Life for me," wrote Hughes, *"ain't been no crystal stair."* I could say the same. I'm sure that's one of the reasons this poem is so dear to me.

We live in a time when life is hard for many people. Yet there is reason to hope and to dig deep for the strength hidden inside of us. That is the message I take from Hughes's poem, and from all the other poems and poets included in this collection. That is also the message I explore in my own poems, inspired by these wonderful wordsmiths of the Harlem Renaissance.

POETRY FORM

The form I used to create this book is called the Golden Shovel. It was first introduced to me when I was asked to contribute to the University of Arkansas Press collection titled *The Golden Shovel Anthology*, a book honoring the work of Gwendolyn Brooks. The poem I penned was titled "Storm," developed from a line in the Brooks poem "A Light and Diplomatic Bird."

The idea of a Golden Shovel poem is to take a short poem in its entirety, or a line from that poem (called a striking line), and create a new poem, using the words from the original. Say you decide to use a single line: you would arrange that line, word by word, in the right margin.

in

the

right

margin.

Then you would write a new poem, each line ending in one of these words. In the example above, that would mean the first line of the new poem would end with the word *in*, the second line would end with the word *the*, and so on.

I wake and shake off the morning as Mom tiptoes **in.**
    "Rise and shine," she whispers, always **the**
        same old song. "Get up. **Right**
    now!" I groan on cue, but she gives me no **margin.**

This is a very challenging way to create a poem, especially in terms of coming up with something that makes sense, and I love it for that very reason! In this form, the poet is bound by the words of the original poem, but the possibilities for creating something entirely new are exciting.

I hope you enjoy reading these as much as I enjoyed writing them!

—Nikki Grimes

PART I

EMERGENCY MEASURES

EMERGENCY MEASURES

by Nikki Grimes

My sister and I watch
the five-o'clock news,
which spells out
our worth in the world.
According to reports,
it's somewhere on the minus side.
That may be only hearsay,
but how can I live long enough
to disprove the lie?
How can I stay strong
in a world where fear and hate
wait outside my door?
My teacher tells me
to go in search of counsel,
back, back, back
to the Harlem Renaissance,
when poetry burst like a dam
and a river of wisdom-words
rushed through the streets
I call home.
Can I really find
fuel for the future
in the past?

Less sure than desperate,
I dip my spoon
into the bowl of years,
stir till I reach the Renaissance
and find a few choice lines
to chew on,
and I think:
We'll see.
We'll see.

Countee Cullen

Langston Hughes

Georgia Douglas Johnson

Paul Laurence Dunbar

Clara Ann Thompson

Gwendolyn Bennett

(William) Waring Cuney

Jean Toomer

STORM ENDING

by Jean Toomer

Thunder blossoms gorgeously above our heads,

Great, hollow, bell-like flowers,

Rumbling in the wind,

Stretching clappers to strike our ears . . .

Full-lipped flowers

Bitten by the sun

Bleeding rain

Dripping rain like golden honey—

And the sweet earth flying from the thunder.

TRUTH

by Nikki Grimes

The truth is, every day we rise is like **thunder—**
a clap of surprise. Could be echoes of trouble, or **blossoms**
of blessing. You never know what garish or **gorgeously**
disguised memories-to-be might rain down from **above.**
So, look up! Claim that cloud with the silver lining. **Our**
job, if you ask me, is to follow it. See where it **heads.**

LIFE AND DEATH

by Clara Ann Thompson

We live, and how intense is life!
So full of stress, so full of strife.
So full of hopes, so full of fears,
Of joy and sorrow, smiles and tears;
And oh how fruitless is the quest,
Unless we're striving for the best.

We die; and oh how sad is death!
How sad, when we relinquish breath,
When all life's glory slips away,
And leaves us but a mass of clay.
How sad, and oh how dark the night,
Unless we've found eternal light!

This, of our brother we can say—
We meet to honor him today,
Because he fought life's battle well;
He stood where heaviest missiles fell.
Oft wounded in the crucial test,
Still, ever striving for the best.

Still striving, he has fallen now,
We've placed the laurel on his brow,
While in our hearts, we wonder why
God called this man so soon to die.

We wonder; oh how blind are we!
His rugged path we could not see;
We only saw his wealth and fame,
His noble station, honored name.
We need not envy him his place,
Who seeks to lift a trodden race.

God knew how hard and well he'd fought,
The noble deeds his hands had wrought;
God heard the deep sighs of his breast,
He heard—and gave the warrior rest.
And shall we weep and say 'tis night,
When he has found eternal light?

CRUCIBLE OF CHAMPIONS

by Nikki Grimes

JAMAR

The evening news never spares us. Tune in and **we**
hear: if you're a boy and you're black, you **live**
with a target on your back. We each take it in **and**
shiver, one sharp-bladed question hanging overhead: **how**
long do I get to walk this earth? The smell of death is too **intense,**
and so we bury the thought, because the future **is**
ours, right? We get to choose? Well, we choose **life.**

DINA

Stupid is the word that stalks me. I'm anything but, **so**
I seethe inside. Even on a good day, I'm **full**
of an anger that burns my breath. Why? It's all because **of**
my diagnosed dyslexia. Ask me to read aloud, I **stress.**
Whenever the teacher calls on me in class, I stutter. **So**
most folks surmise that my head is hollow. Actually, it's quite **full.**
My words and letters simply switch places. They've got a mind **of**
their own. I call that reason enough for stress, for **strife.**

HELENA

I've never met a marine biologist, **so**
what makes me think I could be one? My head is **full**
of fantasies that don't fit other people's ideas **of**
what's possible. They tell me I should squeeze my **hopes**
into a miniature box of their design. But I'm not **so**
inclined. Their infinitesimal perceptions are not for me. I'm **full**
as a piñata, stuffed with daring and delectable dreams **of**
all I can truly be. There's hardly room for doubts, for **fears.**

DAMIAN

No one cuts you any slack if you're a boy, especially **of**
a particular hue, and you decide to find your **joy**
in ballet. Never mind that it's as tough as any sport, **and**
gives you a perfect place to pack whatever **sorrow**
shadows you. Flex, point, leap, and you're all **smiles**
before you know it! Dance is demanding, too, **and**
the strength it takes would leave most jocks in **tears.**

CORA

Lips zipped, I fight to keep silent, to fit in, **and**
when I speak, I whisper. It's silly, I know, but **oh,**
don't the boys love it! Besides, it's **how**
the popular girls behave. It's tiresome, though, even **fruitless,**
to pretend to be somebody you're not. Like Mom says, life **is**
too short. Better to take a lonelier road, discover **the**
who of you. That journey is the best **quest.**

BLAKE

Coach reminds me I'll be stuck in a do-nothing job **unless**
I win one of the basketball scholarships **we're**
all after. Would steroids multiply the effects of my **striving?**
I consider giving them a try, but cheating is not **for**
champions. I'd rather pass the test for the strongest, **the**
fastest, top-notch version of me. Then I'll truly be one of the **best.**

FOR A POET

by Countee Cullen

I have wrapped my dreams in a silken cloth,
And laid them away in a box of gold;
Where long will cling the lips of the moth,
I have wrapped my dreams in a silken cloth;
I hide no hate; I am not even wroth
Who found earth's breath so keen and cold;
I have wrapped my dreams in a silken cloth,
And laid them away in a box of gold.

A SAFE PLACE

by Nikki Grimes

Dream-killers daily stalk the streets you and **I**
travel, trying to trip us up, but we can give them the slip. I **have**
learned to protect my heart-songs. I keep them **wrapped**
in the well wishes of my family, the encouragement of **my**
truest friends. Sometimes, using pen and ink, I anchor my **dreams**
and let them sink in the margins of a diary. Or, maybe I slide them **in**
a smooth sandalwood box buried beneath my bed. But **a**
dream called impossible? That I tuck safely between the **silken**
folds of my private thought—tough as steel, thin as **cloth.**

PART II

CALLING DREAMS

CALLING DREAMS

by Georgia Douglas Johnson

The right to make my dreams come true
I ask, nay, I demand of life,
Nor shall fate's deadly contraband
Impede my steps, nor countermand.

Too long my heart against the ground
Has beat the dusty years around,
And now, at length, I rise, I wake!
And stride into the morning-break!

THE SCULPTOR

by Nikki Grimes

No accident of birth or race or place determines **the**
scope of hope or dreams I have a **right**
to. I inventory my head and heart **to**
weigh and measure what talents I might use to **make**
my own tomorrow. It all depends on the grit at **my**
disposal. My father says hard work is the clay **dreams**
are molded from. Yes. Molded. Dreams do not **come.**
They are carved, muscled into something solid, something **true.**

WE WEAR THE MASK

by Paul Laurence Dunbar

We wear the mask that grins and lies,
It hides our cheeks and shades our eyes,—
This debt we pay to human guile;
With torn and bleeding hearts we smile,
And mouth with myriad subtleties.

Why should the world be overwise,
In counting all our tears and sighs?
Nay, let them only see us, while
    We wear the mask.

We smile, but, O great Christ, our cries
To thee from tortured souls arise.
We sing, but oh the clay is vile
Beneath our feet, and long the mile;
But let the world dream otherwise,
    We wear the mask.

JABARI UNMASKED

by Nikki Grimes

Fresh out of middle school, **we**
all understand the rules: **wear**
whatever's *in*, scowl on cue to convince **the**
world we're fearless—anything to **mask**
the million insecurities **that**
pockmark our skin like acne. Gone the **grins**
when we strut down the hall. We talk tough **and**
hope to God it's enough to get us by. It's all **lies.**

We despise the masquerade. **It**
may disguise our fears, but also **hides**
our kind and tender hearts, **our**
agile minds, the wit that sits behind our **cheeks—**
who'd guess that some of us are geeks **and**
nerds and poets, too? Clothed in **shades**
of chocolate skin, our color works to camouflage **our**
character and promise—at least, in certain **eyes.**

One look, and we are neatly judged **this**
gang, these thugs, these dark delinquents in **debt**
to society. Meanwhile, you fail to see that **we**
are college-bound (more than a few), prepared to **pay**
attention to psychology, the sciences, the arts, **to**
thoughtfully unfurl the scrolls of **human**
history. Instead, you see a thief who uses **guile.**

Is such unfairness what the world is filled **with?**
The evidence is seen in spirits ripped and **torn.**
Still, the world needs the dreams we offer, **and**
should we leave those dreams **bleeding**
on the road, we'd shrink our own **hearts**
down to nothing, and *that* **we**
would regret. Better to let our anger go, and **smile.**

The ignorant ignore as best you can, **and**
in the end, mask aside, freshen your **mouth**
with ferocious lines of potent poetry, **with**
metaphors that mightily reveal the **myriad**
of emotions you feel—yet, in all their **subtleties.**

MOTHER TO SON

by Langston Hughes

Well, son, I'll tell you:
Life for me ain't been no crystal stair.
It's had tacks in it,
And splinters,
And boards torn up,
And places with no carpet on the floor—
Bare.
But all the time
I'se been a-climbin' on,
And reachin' landin's,
And turnin' corners,
And sometimes goin' in the dark
Where there ain't been no light.
So, boy, don't you turn back.
Don't you set down on the steps
'Cause you finds it's kinder hard.
Don't you fall now—
For I'se still goin', honey,
I'se still climbin',
And life for me ain't been no crystal stair.

LESSONS

by Nikki Grimes

Withered and wise, I might as **well**
sift memory for the hard lessons you, my **son,**
most need to learn, though how **I'll**
choose which stories to **tell**—
well . . . I'll just share a few with **you.**

I roll out the years of my **life,**
step carefully, looking out **for**
Daddy, who'd drink, then try to skin **me**
six ways from Sunday. Lord! I **ain't**
had it easy. From birth, my days have **been**
choked with an endless rope of **No**—
no bread in the pantry, no meat, no **crystal**
slipper like the one Cinderella left on that **stair.**

Once, Sheriff pounded on our door. **It's**
day before Christmas, and he **had**
come, waving a notice to lock us out—words sharp as **tacks.**
I prayed under my breath, welcomed him **in**
with tears and kindness. Notice went missing. Never did find **it.**

Work was hard to come by for our kind, **and**
I scrubbed floors till my palms were beds for **splinters.**

Threw my back out one year, **and**
had to sleep on wooden **boards,**
the only way to ease muscles strained and **torn.**
Still, come morn, I was glad for work and reason to get **up.**

Home was nothin' but two rooms **and**
a pull-out bed, though there were worse **places.**
Least we had cupboards **with**
a little somethin' inside. **No**
steak on the table, or rich man's **carpet**
'neath our feet, but still. We kept the heat **on,**
and we'd throw dance parties for rent when **the**
money got tight, push back the sofa and clear the **floor.**

Truth? Life can be sadder than a willow stripped **bare.**

Empty pockets turn you inside out, **but,**
Son, don't mind what's missing. Count **all**
that's free: friendship, laughter, all **the**
love your heart can carry, and time—count **time.**

Busted heart near took me out of here, 'cept **I'se**
too stubborn to leave ahead of the plans I **been**
making to see you fully grown and **a-climbin'**
your *own* stair. Till then, best I just keep **on.**

Life's stair twists, rises, scrapes the sky, **and**
there's light ahead worth **reachin'.**
Aches or no, year by year, I clear the **landin's.**

Son, them nights you serenade me, off-key, **and**
spin me 'cross the floor, **turnin'**
my smile on, help me round rough **corners.**

Last month, power shut off, again, **and**
I bumped round, scrambling for matches. **Sometimes**
I light birthday candles 'fore you can get **goin'**
with a good cry, 'cause you're scared. I start **in**
singing "Happy Birthday" to me, like **the**
lights are out just so the candles can shine in the **dark.**

Hate goin' without power, but what if we lived **where**
women got no rights? Kids work the mines? **There**
are worse things than no lights. **Ain't**
you heard your grandma's stories? She **been**
down South, back when folks like us had **no**
chance to vote, or walk free, even in the day**light.**

A body gets tired, climbin', **so**
you rest every once in a while—hear me, **boy?**
Take a few deep breaths so you **don't**
collapse along the way. **You**
watch how I pace myself, how I **turn**
stubborn instead of turning **back.**

Went to Washington once, **don't**
expect you'd remember. **You**
were just a peanut then. The minute I **set**
foot on the steps of the Lincoln Memorial, **down**
came hot tears, streaking my cheeks, falling **on**
my collar, all because Mr. Lincoln was **the**
one saw to it you and me could plan our own **steps.**

Didn't always like school, 'cause
this one girl, stocky as **you,**
would snatch my books and run till she **finds**
a mud puddle to drop them in. Life—**it's**
full of mean people, but also **kinder**
ones who clean your books 'fore the mud dries **hard.**

No matter what, **don't**
let a few mean people shake **you**
till your young dreams lose their feathers and **fall.**
Hide those baby dreams in the cage of your heart—for **now.**

Your mama's got a surprise **for**
you: withered as I am, **I'se**
got a dream or two, **still,**
a itch my heart keeps scratchin', **goin'**
after like a bee on the hunt for **honey.**

Life's stairway got dips, spirals. **I'se**
dizzy, sometimes, foot-sore and faint. **Still,**
long as there's breath in me, I'll be **climbin'.**

I feel the tug of tomorrow, **and**
grab hold of the railing of **Life.**
Can't guess what's left **for**
me to find, do, be. But hear **me,**
Son, I'm climbin' on, and I **ain't**
leaving you behind. We **been**
bred of sturdy stuff, and **no**
rough times'll stop us. Don't need no **crystal**
slipper to reach the top of the **stair!**

AS THE EAGLE SOARS

by Jean Toomer

It takes a well-spent lifetime, and perhaps more, to crystallize in us
   that for which we exist.

Let your doing be an exercise, not an exhibition.

Man is a nerve of the cosmos, dislocated, trying to quiver into place.

A true individual is not conformative but formative.

We move and hustle but lack rhythm.

We should have a living spirit and the ability to spiritualize experience.

We do not suffer: seldom does our essence suffer, but pride, vanity,
   egotism suffer in us.

My breathing is the Great Breath broken into nostrils.

Whatever is, is sacred.

NO HAMSTERS HERE

by Nikki Grimes

Son, it is all too easy to **let**
this world's bullies puncture **your**
pride, set you on a wild-goose chase of **doing**
whatever crazy thing it takes to "show them." Don't **be**
a hamster on that wheel. We real men know it's only **an**
exercise in futility. Shake off any insults. **Exercise**
your unique talents to learn, grow, be your best—**not**
to prove anything to anyone, though that may well be **an**
added benefit! Life is an art, Son, not an **exhibition.**

An excerpt from **TO USWARD**

by Gwendolyn Bennett

Let us be still
As ginger jars are still
Upon a Chinese shelf,
And let us be contained
By entities of Self . . .

Not still with lethargy and sloth,
But quiet with the pushing of our growth;
Not self-contained with smug identity,
But conscious of the strength in entity.

IN SEARCH OF A SUPERPOWER

by Nikki Grimes

Children, umbrage has its place, but sometimes we must **let**
small injustices and the casual spray of invective spit at **us**
roll off our backs. My grandma would say, "We **be**
better than such meanness. Show hatred the door and be **still."**

A calm demeanor may masquerade **as**
weakness, but looks deceive. Uncut **ginger**
appears an ordinary, worthless root, till opened **jars**
of it infuse the air with a tang so strong, you **are**
bound to blink. Hours later, its power lingers **still.**

On difficult days, gather your resources in silence. Rely **upon**
the perfect, poetic justice history always has **a**
way of delivering. The ancients—Africans, **Chinese—**
knew how to master patience, leave small annoyances on a **shelf.**

I know inner strength is an old man's game, **and**
you are young yet, but this life won't **let**
you hang on to your innocence, any more than it let **us.**
The world can be a dangerous place, and you must **be**
prepared to face it with more grace, less swagger. **Contained**

power is the goal. The mean strut you naturally come **by**
gives too much away. Superman, Wonder Woman—these **entities**
disguised their true might, understanding the advantage **of**
hiding their abilities in plain sight. Each maintained a secret **self**

until those moments when his or her controlled force—**not**
fury—was required. They were the model of cool. **Still**
at times, Clark Kent could play clumsy. Even so, **with**
his zeal for truth and news, none would accuse him of **lethargy.**
He moved fast enough to stay ahead of the game, **and**
you must too. Walk with measured steps, always intent. Even the **sloth**

has purpose. Ha! Wish I understood that when I was young, **but**
I was all brash-and-stomp back then, never **quiet,**
never noticing how or where I stepped, or **with**
whom. (Not all movement is forward.) Better to be like **the**
tree, grounding itself by sinking roots downward, while **pushing**
upward through hard-packed earth, in search **of**
sun—all done silently, mysteriously, right before **our**
eyes. Confidence can rise as stealthily as the redwood's **growth!**

Cockiness is something else, altogether, a thing **not**
to be emulated. Better an easy laugh and a pride **self-contained.**
Any thug can pretend manliness **with**
a crude swagger, a nasty smirk, or a **smug**
attitude. Mark my word: rudeness makes for a poor **identity.**

Stand tall, head held high at all times, **but** bow humbly when the occasion warrants. Be **conscious** of the treasure of your mind and heart, the pride **of** your ancestry, the debt you owe those who came before. **The** future requires steadiness, perseverance, **strength—** gifts you access with the key of your will. The power you seek is **in** sight. Look in the mirror. Own yourself. You are that **entity.**

HOPE

by Georgia Douglas Johnson

Frail children of sorrow, dethroned by a hue,
The shadows are flecked by the rose sifting through,
The world has its motion, all things pass away,
No night is omnipotent, there must be day.

The oak tarries long in the depth of the seed,
But swift is the season of nettle and weed,
Abide yet awhile in the mellowing shade,
And rise with the hour for which you were made.

The cycle of seasons, the tidals of man
Revolve in the orb of an infinite plan,
We move to the rhythm of ages long done,
And each has his hour—to dwell in the sun!

ON BULLY PATROL

by Nikki Grimes

1.

My youngest limps home, feeble and **frail**
from a week of hate-filled reproaches aimed at dark **children.**
I pull her close, wipe away the tears **of**
the day. Still, draped in sadness, **sorrow**
clings to her like skin. My sweet princess, **dethroned.**
I shape my love like fingers, pluck the splinters of hate, one **by**
one, until my child smiles again, **a**
glow rising in her warm, brown cheeks—a happy **hue.**

2.

My six-year-old self remembers the sting of slurs, **the**
hurt that rubbed raw, sent me to the company of **shadows.**
Call it the terror of "too." If you **are**
too dark, too skinny, too tall—too whatever, you'll be **flecked**
with pellets of meanness, most always **by**
bullies with wounds of their own. I've seen **the**
scars they hide, each jagged as a red-**rose**
thorn. "You'll be fine," I tell my youngest, **sifting**
my own memories, seeing how the light shines **through.**

3.

Long ago, war snatched my Daddy, tore **the**
heart out of Mama, out of our **world.**
Thought I'd crack from the weight of hurt, but time **has**
a way of teaching that life finds **its**
own balance. It swings up, swings down. The **motion**
sweeps us along, notwithstanding—we **all**
suffer bad days. When tears threaten, breathe. **Things**
will lift, like morning mist. By and by, you'll **pass**
over each bridge of trouble, see the sadness drift **away.**

4.

I watch my youngest leap like gravity's got **no**
hold on her. You'd never guess there was a **night**
she took sick, her spirit rising near to heaven as the sun **is.**
I scraped my knees raw, pleading with the **Omnipotent**
One. Got the answer I was after, or **there**
would be no me, laughing at my daughter's antics. "You **must**
remember to give thanks," I tell my girls. "**Be**
grateful that darkness burns to ash in the flame of **day.**"

5.

My eldest, too like me, payment for **the**
pain I caused my mother because I was stubborn as **oak.**
Worse yet—again, like me—my first child **tarries**
over each assigned task far too **long,**
ever seeking impossible perfection **in**
the doing of it. Never mind that **the**
symmetry she desires is beyond human **depth.**
I sigh, recalling the ultimate value **of**
such doggedness, the strength implied, **the**
sturdy beauty of a stubborn **seed.**

6.

Notice, traits of beauty tend to inch along in growth. **But**
habits mean and horrible are devilishly **swift**
to sprout and spread. The splitting of the truth **is**
one such to avoid. Plant a false word at dawn, **the**
lie is harvested by noon, no matter the **season.**
Nail-biting may be harmless, but beware **of**
tendencies to cheat. A bad habit, like a **nettle,**
leaves a scratch upon the soul, **and**
who needs that? A bad habit is an ugly **weed.**

7

Friday arrives with the promise that my husband will **abide**
with his girls for more than a minute. **Yet**
one can't be certain work won't steal him **awhile.**
Come Saturday, though, he dons a grilling apron **in**
the evening, and sends savory scents wafting into **the**
summer air. "Count these times precious, girls—Dad **mellowing**
in the yard, then chasing your mama for a kiss in the **shade."**

8.

Intent on peering into tomorrow, I squint **and**
wonder who my girls will grow to be, how they'll **rise**
to find their place in the sky. "Begin **with**
whatever makes your heart sing," I teach them, "**the**
dream that clings to you every **hour.**
That's the key to what you're here **for."**
To write? Dance? Build bridges? **Which**
is an itch in your soul? I'll tell **you**
a secret: Your longings **were**
already carefully carved, your true purpose long ago **made.**

9.

My eldest, anxious to lean into **the**
dark abyss of the teen years, begins the **cycle**
in a terrible hurry to date. But I am **of**
a mind to make her wait awhile. The **seasons**
of life already swing by faster than **the**
hem of a hurricane. Hard to explain **tidals**
to one who's never gotten her feet wet, **of**
course. Still, she's too young for the arms of a **man.**

10.

When I was her age, my thoughts did not **revolve**
around boys. Education was the thing on my mind **in**
those days. Mom harped so on learning, by high school **the**
whole of my cerebrum was an **orb**
stuffed with history, geometry, and the plays **of**
Shakespeare. Earning a place in **an**
accredited college and graduating with honors was of **infinite**
importance. As for the cost? Daddy said he had a **plan.**

11.

I must teach my girls how, uncelebrated, **we**
lay tomorrow, brick by brick, **move**
forward through wind and storm, from winter **to**
winter, often without benefit of praise, or **the**
occasional pat on the back. We sweat to the **rhythm**
of sunrise and sunset. Hard work? Never heard **of**
another kind. Grandparents taught us as much **ages**
ago. Now it's our turn to pass it on. Before **long,**
a future built of sweat and dreams will, finally, be **done.**

12.

Today I remind them that hate-filled reproaches **and**
mean-mouthed people have no real power. **Each**
living soul, no matter the hue, **has**
the right to choose her path, or **his.**
We heal or wound, build or break, make of each **hour**
what we will. Choice is our treasure. It is up **to**
us, when tempted to swell in anger, to **dwell**
instead in peace, wherever we can find it. **In**
time we discover that **the**
path of right always leads to light, to **sun.**

THE NEGRO SPEAKS OF RIVERS

by Langston Hughes

I've known rivers:

I've known rivers ancient as the world and older than the

flow of human blood in human veins.

My soul has grown deep like the rivers.

I bathed in the Euphrates when dawns were young.

I built my hut near the Congo and it lulled me to sleep.

I looked upon the Nile and raised the pyramids above it.

I heard the singing of the Mississippi when Abe Lincoln

went down to New Orleans, and I've seen its muddy

bosom turn all golden in the sunset.

I've known rivers:

Ancient, dusky rivers.

My soul has grown deep like the rivers.

DAVID'S OLD SOUL

by Nikki Grimes

As far back as I can remember, **my**
mother has called me "an old **soul."**
I never understood. But now that our family **has**
dwindled to just Mom and us kids, I've **grown**
into a man. You do what you have to. "David, dig **deep,"**
is the whisper in my ear. So I stand strong **like**
a tree my baby brothers can lean on. I try to be **the**
raft that helps carry them over this life's rough **rivers.**

PART III

TO A DARK GIRL

TO A DARK GIRL

by Gwendolyn Bennett

I love you for your brownness
And the rounded darkness of your breast.
I love you for the breaking sadness in your voice
And shadows where your wayward eye-lids rest.

Something of old forgotten queens
Lurks in the lithe abandon of your walk,
And something of the shackled slave
Sobs in the rhythm of your talk.

Oh, little brown girl, born for sorrow's mate,
Keep all you have of queenliness,
Forgetting that you once were slave,
And let your full lips laugh at Fate!

THROUGH THE EYES OF ARTISTS

by Nikki Grimes

ARIANA

Your complexion cries out for brush and canvas. **I**
rush to gather raw umber, yellow ochre, the Indian red I **love,**
pondering the perfect blend to capture **you**
in this moment, certainly, but also **for**
eternity. Perplexed, you're unable to fathom my fire, **your**
worth. Who has taught you to disdain your **brownness?**

Never mind. I will teach you otherwise **and**
prove with lush layers of paint and pastel **the**
true appeal of dusky brown, multiplied and **rounded**
off to the nth degree, deep as the **darkness**
of the night sky we all speak **of**
in whispers of awe. How you glow, **your**
inner light as pure as the milk from a mother's **breast!**

Quickly, I brandish my brush, stab the canvas with colors **I**
have blended to bloom before your eyes, to make you **love**
yourself again. See the blue undertones? The hint of purple **you**
have to squint to recognize? The touch of burnt sienna **for**
warmth, the wash of crimson beneath the cheeks? **The**

slim stroke of sepia is there too, **breaking**

just beneath the eyes, marking the **sadness**

hidden there, in the soft folds. Yes, there is beauty even **in**

sadness. Think of a symphony in a minor key, how **your**

heart soars with the sorrowful moan of each instrument's **voice.**

All right. The background set, I move on to the shading, **and**

carve the curve of each cheek, the sweep of nose with **shadows.**

A wash of Van Dyck Brown does the trick. But **where**

will I find the color that will saturate **your**

soul, paint a smile on your face, replace that lost and **wayward**

glance with easy confidence? I sigh, but in the end, your **eye-lids**

lift to view your brown beauty. And you smile, all doubt put to **rest.**

SOPHIA

Your limbs were made for leaping, yet **something**

binds you to the earth, some lash made **of**

history halts your steps, slows you like an **old**

crone. Step lively! Straighten your spine! Have you **forgotten**

you come from African kings and **queens?**

The false notion that you are nothing **lurks**

deep in the bone. Let's beat it out **in**

dance! Fling your arms skyward. Flick **the**

lie from your fingertips. Remember: your brown limbs are **lithe**

and lovely. Now leap! Arch your back! Dance with **abandon!**

Own your body and your mind. Let nothing resembling limitation **of**
spirit or possibility define the way you hold **your**
body, the way you **walk.**

You are young, yet I have seen you bowed **and**
shuffling. No more! Glide! Strut! Keep your eyes pinned on **something**
bright and blossoming up ahead, a future sculpted **of**
dreams and promise. That is what **the**
Freedom Riders fought for, that you need not live **shackled**
by another's narrow estimation. (There are many ways to be a **slave.)**

Spin! That's it! Let your limbs laugh. **Sobs**
belong to yesterday. Time to trade them **in**
for jazz hands or hip-swivels, or arabesques, **the**
best expression of freedom. Let the **rhythm**
of dance transport you to a tomorrow **of**
noble design. Dip. Yes! Now lunge! Discover where **your**
true potential pulses. All action. No **talk.**

TONYA

Your life's story is a tale worth telling. **Oh,**
others try to squeeze it down into the **little**
crevices of history where they imagine all **brown**
stories belong. But pay them no mind, **girl;**
I will ink the extraordinary story only you were **born**
with. Trading tales is what we're meant **for,**

whether marking our joy's or our **sorrow's**
sameness. Brown or not, every story has its **mate.**

All right! My pen is at the ready. I'll **keep**
it moving to the meter of your words till **all**
the metaphors necessary to describe **you,**
from timidities to talents, **have**
found their way into whatever pocket **of**
verse seems most suited. **Queenliness**

seems a fitting beginning. No, I'm not **forgetting**
the tenement you live in, but **that,**
my friend, is where you reside, not what **you**
are made of. I was told, **once,**
that true nobility is the crown of character. You **were**
royal from your first kind word. Never were you a **slave**

to meanness. Stubborn? Yes, **and**
always sarcastic. That is, until you **let**
your guard down. Then **your**
heart hums sweetly as a music box **full**
of soothing melody, and your **lips**
offer a world of welcome in a smile, a **laugh,**
no matter how difficult your day. Is that not worth noting? **At**
the end of your story, you're strong enough to write your own **Fate.**

COMMON DUST

by Georgia Douglas Johnson

And who shall separate the dust
Which later we shall be:
Whose keen discerning eye will scan
And solve the mystery?

The high, the low, the rich, the poor,
The black, the white, the red,
And all the chromatique between,
Of whom shall it be said:

Here lies the dust of Africa;
Here are the sons of Rome;
Here lies one unlabelled
The world at large his home!

Can one then separate the dust,
Will mankind lie apart,
When life has settled back again
The same as from the start?

A DARK DATE FOR JOSH

by Nikki Grimes

Proud as anything, I march into the house **and**
tell Mom that Tanisha is my date for the prom. "**Who?**"
she asks, shuddering like lightning struck her. "You **shall**
not!" she says, without a trace of humor to **separate**
her words from her meaning. Right away I guess **the**
ugly reason and stomp out, mouth dry as **dust.**

I choke on words Mom used to say. *We're all alike.* **Which**
is it, Mom? Blood steaming, I could scream. Maybe **later.**
Now I stare at a photo of Tanisha and me, see how perfect **we**
are. I don't much like Mom at the moment, with her silly "**shall**
not." She's got me worried about what Dad's response will **be.**

At dinner Dad spies upset on my face, and Mom's. "**Whose**
dog died?" he asks, straining for laughter, **keen**
to lift the mood like a feather, toss it into the air. **Discerning**
the tension in the room, he turns an **eye**
on Mom, hoping for answers, realizing no joke **will**
do the trick. His stare probes deep as any X-ray **scan.**

Dad looks from Mom, to me, to Mom, **and**
back again. "Unless I know the problem, I can't **solve**
it," he says. I count to ten, then, "I'm taking Tanisha to **the**
prom," I say in a rush, ending the **mystery.**

Will he implode like Mom? Forget all **the**
lessons he's taught me about equality? Desert the **high**
ideals he preaches? "I don't understand," he says. "Is **the**
girl an ax murderer? Do you know her to be of **low**
morals? What?" I exhale, long and slow, feel **the**
sweet tug of a smile teasing my lips, hear the **rich,**
righteous *Exactly!* explode in my brain. *That's* **the**
dad I know. But Mom's once-generous spirit seems suddenly **poor.**

I open memory like a book and find **the**
boy I played with next door, the friend who was less **black**
than mocha and cream. We seemed like two sides of **the**
same coin all through grade school, and my **white**
family liked his black family just fine. Mom always said **the**
blood that flows through our veins is exactly the same: **red.**

She should know. She runs the neighborhood beauty shop **and**
prides herself on being the primary colorist **all**
the ladies ask for, black or white. She understands **the**
alchemy of hue. Brunette or brightest blond, at Salon **Chromatique**
my mom lays hands on any and every color in **between.**

From what I've seen, she gets along with all **of**
her customers, pink-cheeked or chocolate, at least those **whom**
I've met. I don't get how she could sing, "We **Shall**
Overcome" alongside some of our neighbors, then lose **it**
the minute a brown beauty like Tanisha catches my eye. **Be**
consistent, Mom. Do what you've taught. Live what you've **said.**

Eyes closed, Mom peels back the years, leaves the **here**
and now, explains the knot of fear that clearly **lies**
inside her. "When I was your age, I went to **the**
prom with a boy as dark as Mississippi **dust.**
It was just a dance, so I thought nothing **of**
it, till someone spit at us and yelled, 'Boy, go back to **Africa!'"**

I shiver, but say, "It's not like that anymore. Not **here."**
Dad's eyes say otherwise. "I'm afraid there **are**
roiling waves of racism in every generation. **The**
present is no different. Still, I won't have any **sons**
of mine surrender to the bitter current **of**
the past. Let it ebb away, recede like the power of **Rome."**

Silence pulls up a chair and sits **here**
like it belongs. Unease is the only thing that **lies**
between us. I hate these talks, wish there were only **one**
race, that we could live the way we were born—**unlabelled.**

Then we'd have no excuse to use **the**
shape of eye or nose, or hue of skin to carve the **world**
into a million meaningless categories **at**
first sight. Maybe then we might see that the planet is **large**
enough for everyone to fit, for each to find **his**
own someone, his own place, his own **home.**

In school, we dissect frogs to see what we **can**
learn. Funny how, on the inside, you can't tell **one**
frog from the other. Another lesson wasted if you **then**
run from anyone who seems unlike you. Why can't we wait to **separate,**
to crawl into a cocoon of those wrapped in similar skin? In **the**
end, every one of us is guaranteed to be just … **dust.**

When our bodies are bloodless and still, who **will**
identify which bone came from canine, and which from **mankind?**
When Time grinds us fine as grain, and we **lie**
without skin or bone or heart, who'll be able to tell us **apart?**

I think these things but don't speak. Later, after dinner, **when**
I help Mom clear the table, she sneaks in a hug, says, "Your **life**
is your own, Son. Forget about my fears. Your heart **has**
to find its own home." I smile and tell her, now that it's **settled,**
"We're just going to prom, Mom—not getting married." She smiles **back**
and, suddenly, we're our old selves **again.**

I call Tanisha before turning in, tell her about all **the**
hubbub at my house. Find out she went through the **same.**
We laugh, an edge in both of our voices. We act **as**
if neither notices. We talk particulars, like where to go **from**
prom. From here. I can't tell Mom, but this isn't just a date. **The**
prom is more like a test run for my heart. It's—a **start.**

NO IMAGES

by Waring Cuney

She does not know
Her beauty,
She thinks her brown body
Has no glory.

If she could dance
Naked,
Under palm trees
And see her image in the river
She would know.

But there are no palm trees
On the street,
And dish water gives back no images.

BLURRED BEAUTY

by Nikki Grimes

Today I trembled, jealous of the book **she**
cradled close to her heart like a baby, the way a mother **does.**
Lily. I haven't even said her name out loud. **Not**
yet. But it's tattooed on my soul. One day, she'll **know.**

Maybe tomorrow I'll speak, tell her to raise her head, lift **her**
eyes, invite the world to swim in their dark **beauty.**

I hate how Lily always hugs the wall, how **she**
pretends to be invisible. She **thinks,**
or hopes, no one will notice **her,**
but who can miss all that velvety chocolate-**brown**
deliciousness? The sun is not the only heavenly **body.**

I wonder if she's ever been kissed, if any lucky boy **has**
brushed those lips with his? I hope the answer is **no.**
It's my heart she holds. Lily's first kiss should be my **glory.**

Look how she hangs her head, as **if**
she weren't born a queen, as if **she**
doesn't know she could rule with a smile, **could**
lift one little finger and make the whole world **dance.**

That's the pure truth. All of it. **Naked.**

Queen Lily. Can you see her, lying on a beach, **under**
a scorching sun, royal guard cooling her with a fan of **palm**
leaves? Everyone and everything bows to her, even the **trees.**

She rises from a short nap **and**
walks to the crystal water's edge to **see**
if she can find a shell that holds an echo, that sings in **her**
ear. But all the water offers the queen is her own **image,**
surrounded by a halo of sky, lovely **in**
its symmetry. Burnished by **the**
sun, Queen Lily dives into the cool of the **river.**

Yeah, I'm a dreamer. But Lily, **she**
brings that out in me. If you saw her, you **would**
understand. You would **know.**

I whistled at Lily when she passed by today, **but**
she didn't turn or look up to see me, standing **there.**
I wonder: Does she stare in the puddles when it rains? **Are**
there mirrors in her house that show her what I see? **No**
one with such luscious lips should ever cover them with the **palm**
of her hand. Hold your head high, Lily. Stand proud as **trees.**

Ignore those fast-talking, know-nothing guys **on**
the avenue, describing you with **the**
twisted words self-hate taught them on the **street.**

Tomorrow. Tomorrow I'll speak **and**
I'll whip you up a gourmet **dish**
of compliments, sweet words you can use to **water**
the garden of your mind. I'll find a clear pool that **gives**
you a true reflection of sturdy brown legs, gently swayed **back,**
the black brows that frame eyes I want to drown in, and—**no.**
I'll just show you my heart. Look there. Study the **images.**

THE MINOR KEY

by Clara Ann Thompson

"Oh for a song" the poet sighs,
"To stir men's hearts and make them rise
    To heights of nobleness!
A song whose clarion notes will ring,
Long after I have ceased to sing,
    And heal life's bitterness.
Alas! this is the fate for me:
To ever sing in a minor key."

A thousand hearts echo the sigh,
    Brave hearts that struggle on alone,
With aspirations pure and high,
    With deeds forgotten or unknown.

They hear the proud world laud the great,
    They watch the cheering crowds go by,
And bitterly lament their fate—
    Oh foolish hearts, subdue that cry!

What matter if the world forgets,
   Thy deeds to laud, thy tale to tell?
   If God remembers, all is well;
With Him who sees not as we see,
No life is tuned to minor key.

COMMON DENOMINATOR

by Nikki Grimes

Anger is a hard itch to scratch; laughter **a**
secret tickle we let out in a **thousand**
sneezes, sometimes to camouflage cracked **hearts;**
love, envy, fear—we all hear their **echo.**
Peel us to the core, we're indistinguishable. Press **the**
solar plexus of any, you'll hear the selfsame **sigh.**

WHATEVER MAKES YOUR
HEART
SING

I LEAVE THE GLORY DAYS

by Nikki Grimes

I leave the glory days
of the Harlem Renaissance,
swim to the surface of
the bowl of years,
and take a sweet breath.
Standing taller than ever,
I feel full of something
strange and delicious:
hope.
Teacher was right.
The past is a ladder
that can help you
keep climbing.
I find my sister
in the living room,
surprise her with a tight squeeze
and a swing into the air.
"We're going to be all right, Sis,"
I whisper.
"You and me,
we're going to be okay."
I know life will be rough,
but we've got the stuff
to make it.

RESOURCES

POET BIOGRAPHIES

 GWENDOLYN BENNETT, 1902–1981

Born in Giddings, Texas, Bennett attended Columbia University, graduated from Pratt Institute, and taught art at Howard University. Awarded a scholarship to study art at the Sorbonne, she left Howard briefly but resumed teaching upon her return from Paris. Based in Harlem, Bennett had a passion for black art and literature that led her to become the assistant editor of the magazine *Opportunity*, in which she wrote the literary column "The Ebony Flute." When editor Charles S. Johnson introduced the group he referred to as "The Younger School of Negro Writers" at the famous Civic Club dinner during the Harlem Renaissance, Bennett was among them, offering a special poem dedicated to the occasion. Bennett's poetry frequently appeared in literary magazines and journals, and was featured in Alain Locke's seminal anthology, *The New Negro.* Bennett never published a poetry collection of her own, but was influential in promoting, nurturing, and publishing Langston Hughes and other notable poets of the era. A member of the Harlem Artists Guild and director of the Harlem Community Art Center from 1939–1944, Bennett remained active in the arts throughout her life.

COUNTEE CULLEN, 1903-1946

Raised in New York, Countee Cullen spread his poetry wings early in life, winning a citywide poetry contest while still a schoolboy. He later graduated from New York University (1925), received his master's from Harvard (1926), and, between the two, published *Color,* his first collection of poetry. An assistant editor for the magazine *Opportunity*, Cullen wrote a monthly column called "The Dark Tower" and quickly rose as a leading voice of the Harlem Renaissance. He published the novel *One Way to Heaven* and several poetry collections, including *Copper Sun* (1927), *The Ballad of the Brown Girl* (1927), and *The Black Christ and Other Poems* (1929). From 1934 to his death, Cullen shared his love of literature with the next generation as a teacher in the New York City public schools. The Countee Cullen Library, located in Harlem, is named in his honor.

Selected Works:

Color (1925); *Copper Sun* (1927); *The Ballad of the Brown Girl* (1927); *The Black Christ and Other Poems* (1929); *One Way to Heaven*, a novel (1932); *The Medea and Some Poems* (1935); *The Lost Zoo* (1940); *My Lives and How I Lost Them* (1942); *On These I Stand* (1947)

(WILLIAM) WARING CUNEY, 1906-1976

William Waring Cuney, born in Washington, DC, studied music at the New England Conservatory of Music and at the Conservatory of Music in Rome before switching his focus from singing to sonnets. This now seems destined, though, since "No Images," a poem he penned at age eighteen, was to become the most anthologized and translated poem associated with the Harlem Renaissance. Winner of a prize in an *Opportunity* magazine literary competition, "No Images" remains Cuney's most famous poem. In 1941, Cuney's worlds of music and poetry came together when performer Josh White recorded his poems on the album *Southern Exposure*, and later when Nina Simone set "No Images" to music for her album *Let It All Out*. In 1960 Cuney produced *Puzzles*, a limited-edition poetry collection published by a Dutch literary society. He then retreated from public life until 1972. A year later Cuney's second poetry collection, *Storefront Church*, was published in London.

Selected Works:
Puzzles (1960); *Storefront Church* (1973)

 PAUL LAURENCE DUNBAR, 1872–1906
Born in Dayton, Ohio, Paul Laurence Dunbar was the first nationally recognized African American poet. This son of former slaves got an early start, editing a black newspaper in high school and publishing poems in the *Dayton Herald* by the age of fourteen. In 1893 he self-published his first book of poetry, *Oak and Ivy*, and by 1895 his verse had appeared in the pages of the *New York Times*. He was known for writing in heavy black dialect, though he

also wrote in an elegant, lyrical style. By 1897 his popularity made it possible for him to go on a six-month poetry-reading tour in England. Though his work predates the Harlem Renaissance, Dunbar proved that national—and even international—recognition for an African American poet was possible. This prolific writer produced eight collections of poetry, a novel (*The Uncalled*), a short story collection *(Folks from Dixie)*, and numerous song lyrics before his death at age thirty-three. In 1913 a collection of Dunbar's verse was published in the book *The Complete Poems of Paul Laurence Dunbar.* "We Wear the Mask" is one of his best-known poems.

Selected Works:
Oak and Ivy (1893); *Majors and Minors* (1895); *Lyrics of Lowly Life* (1896); *The Uncalled,* a novel (1898); *Folks from Dixie,* short stories (1898); *Lyrics of the Hearthside, Poems of Cabin and Field* (1899); *Lyrics of Love and Laughter* (1903); *Howdy, Howdy, Howdy* (1905); *Lyrics of Sunshine and Shadow* (1905); *The Complete Poems of Paul Laurence Dunbar* (1913)

LANGSTON HUGHES, 1902–1967
James Mercer Langston Hughes began writing poetry while a young student. Not long after graduating high school, his popular poem "The Negro Speaks of Rivers" was first published in the *Crisis* magazine. In 1925 Hughes entered a poem in *Opportunity* magazine's

literary competition and won first prize for "The Weary Blues." That became the title of his first book of poetry, published by Knopf in 1926. Various novels, plays, short story collections, and other collections of poetry followed, including *The Dream Keeper and Other Poems*, written for young readers. Aside from these works, Hughes also published English translations of poetry by Federico García Lorca and Gabriela Mistral. Through the decades, Hughes's name became synonymous with the Harlem Renaissance. His work is widely published and taught. Schools and libraries across America now bear his name, and his Harlem home is a New York City landmark.

Selected Works:
The Weary Blues (1926); *Fine Clothes to the Jew* (1927*)*; *Dear Lovely Death* (1931); *Scottsboro Limited* (1932); *The Dream Keeper and Other Poems* (1932); *Shakespeare in Harlem* (1942); *Freedom's Plow* (1943); *Fields of Wonder* (1947); *One-Way Ticket* (1949); *Montage of a Dream Deferred* (1951); *Ask Your Mama: 12 Moods for Jazz* (1961); *The Panther and the Lash: Poems of Our Times* (1967); *The Collected Poems of Langston Hughes* (1994)

GEORGIA DOUGLAS JOHNSON, 1880–1966
Born in Atlanta, Georgia, this poet eventually settled in Washington, DC, where she was swept up in the cultural high tide of the Harlem Renaissance as it spread. A playwright, columnist, and poet, Johnson's verse was

first published in the *Crisis* magazine. *The Heart of a Woman*, her first book of poetry, appeared in 1918, to be followed by the popular, racially themed collection *Bronze*, and two others. The musicality of Johnson's work reflects her years of study at Oberlin Conservatory and Cleveland College of Music and may explain why she was one of the young black writers formally introduced to the white literary establishment by editor Charles S. Johnson at the noted Civic Club dinner in 1924. Johnson went on to become the most highly anthologized female poet of the era and, alongside Langston Hughes and Countee Cullen, was among the first black writers included in white mainstream publications like *Harper's* and *Century*. In addition, Johnson's DC home became a popular art salon where Harlem Renaissance writers frequently met to share ideas. In 1965 Atlanta University recognized Johnson's work with an honorary doctorate in literature.

Selected Works:
The Heart of a Woman (1918); *Bronze* (1922); *An Autumn Love Cycle* (1928); *Share My World* (1962)

CLARA ANN THOMPSON, 1869–1949
The daughter of former slaves, Ohio-born Clara Ann Thompson came from a family of artists. Her brother Garland Yancy was a sculptor, while her brother Aaron and sister, Priscilla, both wrote poetry, as Clara did herself. Thompson taught in Ohio public schools during

the day and, in her free time, wrote and gave public readings of her poetry. In 1908 her brother Aaron helped her publish *Songs by the Wayside*, her first book of verse. That collection was followed by *A Garland of Poems*, a book that honored the courageous black soldiers who fought in World War I. This book appeared a year after Alain Locke's *The New Negro* anthology trumpeted the beginning of the Harlem Renaissance. In later years Thompson's work was anthologized in *Collected Black Women's Poetry*; *Afro-American Women Writers 1746–1933*; and *Voices in the Poetic Tradition*, edited by Henry Louis Gates Jr. (1996).

Selected Works:
Songs by the Wayside (1908); *A Garland of Poems* (1926)

JEAN TOOMER, 1894–1967

Jean Toomer, grandson of P. B. S. Pinchback, America's first black governor, made his own mark as one of the country's most brilliant writers. Toomer settled in New York City by 1919, and he accepted a temporary post in Sparta, Georgia, in 1921, working as acting principal in a rural school. By the time he returned north two months later, he had the seeds for the novel *Cane*, a groundbreaking work of fiction about black life in the South. Called experimental fiction, *Cane* wove together poetry, plays, and fiction. It was one of the first books about black life published by the white literary establishment, and became a benchmark for the literature of the Harlem Renaissance. Best known for *Cane*, Toomer produced other novels, as well as countless short stories, essays, plays, and poems. The latter can be found in *The Collected Poems of Jean Toomer*, edited by Robert B. Jones and Margery Toomer Latimer (1988).

Selected Works:

Cane, a novel (1923); *The Gallonwerps,* a play (1927); *York Beach,* a novella (1929); *The Blue Meridian,* an epic poem (1931); *The Angel Begori,* a novel (1940); *The Collected Poems of Jean Toomer* (1988)

ARTIST BIOGRAPHIES

COZBI A. CABRERA's beautiful, handcrafted cloth dolls have garnered the attention of collectors around the world. She has illustrated the books *Beauty, Her Basket; Thanks a Million; Most Loved in All the World;* and *Stitchin' and Pullin': A Gee's Bend Quilt.* She attended Parsons School of Design and lives in Brooklyn, New York. Visit her online at www.cozbi.com. ("The Sculptor," p. 33.)

R. GREGORY CHRISTIE has illustrated more than fifty books for young adults and children and has collaborated with clients such as the *New Yorker, Rolling Stone, Vibe,* the *Wall Street Journal,* the *New York Times,* the Kennedy Center, Marlo Thomas, Pete Seeger, Chris Rock, Queen Latifah, and Karyn Parsons. He is a two-time recipient of the annual *New York Times* 10 Best Illustrated Children's Books Award and a four-time winner of the Coretta Scott King Illustrator Honor Book award. He's also been awarded the Boston Globe–Horn Book Award and the American Library Association's Theodor Seuss Geisel Honor Book award. Mr. Christie currently works as a freelance illustrator and operates his bookstore, GAS-ART GIFTS, which carries autographed children's books, in Decatur, Georgia. For more information, visit www.gas-art.com. ("Truth," p. 17.)

PAT CUMMINGS has authored and illustrated numerous books for young readers and is the editor of the award-winning series Talking with Artists. Her children's book classes at Parsons School of Design and Pratt Institute and her annual Children's Book Boot Camp list a growing number of notable book illustrators and authors among their graduates. She also serves on the boards of the Authors Guild and the Society of Children's Book Writers and Illustrators and is chair of the Society of Illustrators Founder's Award. Her book *Beauty and the Beast* was translated from the original French and retold by her husband, H. Chuku Lee. She lives in Brooklyn, New York. Visit her online at www.patcummings .com. ("David's Old Soul," p. 67.)

JAN SPIVEY GILCHRIST's career as a fine artist has spanned a quarter of a century. She has exhibited extensively throughout the world and won numerous awards throughout her career, including the Coretta Scott King Illustrator Award for *Nathaniel Talking* and a Coretta Scott King Illustrator Honor Book award for *Night on Neighborhood Street*. Ms. Gilchrist has illustrated many of Eloise Greenfield's books, including several award winners. *The Great Migration: Journey to the North* was named a 2012 Coretta Scott King Author Honor Book and an ALA Notable Children's Book, among many other accolades. She is also a winner of the Zora Neale Hurston Award, the highest honor given by the National Association of Black Storytellers, Inc. Ms. Gilchrist and her husband, Dr. Kelvin Gilchrist, live in a suburb of Chicago,

Illinois. Visit her online at www.janspiveygilchrist.com. ("A Dark Date for Josh," p. 83.)

EBONY GLENN is an artist living on the quiet outskirts of Atlanta, Georgia. With an arts degree in drawing and painting from the University of North Georgia, she aspires to bring stories to life with fanciful illustrations that are filled with whimsy and charm, providing rich literary experiences for readers. When Ms. Glenn is not giving in to her creative itch of art-making, you may find her lost in the pages of a good book, learning some new Hula-Hooping tricks, or going on an adventure with her pup, Louie. Visit her online at www.ebonyglenn.com. ("On Bully Patrol," p. 63.)

NIKKI GRIMES, a long-time textile artist, decided to try her hand at visual art as a way to sharpen her faculties. What began as a lark soon became a love. In recent years, her watercolor and mixed media works have been exhibited and sold in several galleries in Southern California. Her contribution to this collection, however, is her first illustration. Visit her online at www.nikkigrimes.com. ("Blurred Beauty," page 89.)

E. B. LEWIS is the acclaimed illustrator of more than fifty books for children, including the Caldecott Honor book *Coming On Home Soon* and several Coretta Scott King Award winners, such as *Talkin' About Bessie: The Story of Aviator Elizabeth Coleman* and *The Bat Boy and His Violin*. He lives in Folsom, New

Jersey. Visit him online at www.eblewis.com. ("Through the Eyes of Artists," p. 75.)

FRANK MORRISON works as a fine artist and is the award-winning illustrator of many books for children, including *I Got the Rhythm*; he is a contributor to *Our Children Can Soar*, and illustrated *Jazzy Miz Mozetta,* for which he won the Coretta Scott King/John Steptoe New Talent Award. Frank lives with his wife and their five children in Atlanta, Georgia. Visit him online at www.morrisongraphics.com. ("A Safe Place," p. 27.)

CHRISTOPHER MYERS is a versatile artist, working with photos, gouache, woodcuts, collage, and other artistic media. He has worked with numerous authors, including his father, noted author Walter Dean Myers, and most recently, Misty Copeland. Myers also codirected the documentary film *Am I Going Too Fast?* with Hank Willis Thomas and has designed for theater. He has written several notable essays, among them: "Young Dreamers," an eloquent reflection on Trayvon Martin and Ezra Jack Keats' *The Snowy Day*, and, most famously, the much-discussed "The Apartheid of Children's Literature," which ran in the *New York Times* in 2014. His works of fine art have been exhibited at MoMA PS1; Contrasts Gallery in Shanghai; the last Prospect Biennial in New Orleans; and in the exhibition Art of Jazz, recently featured at the Cooper Gallery at Harvard. He lives in Brooklyn, New York. ("Lessons," p. 45.)

BRIAN PINKNEY is the acclaimed illustrator of several highly praised picture books, including *The Faithful Friend*, *In the Time of the Drums*, and *Duke Ellington*. Brian has won numerous awards, including Caldecott Honors, Coretta Scott King Honors, a Coretta Scott King Illustrator Award, and a Boston Globe–Horn Book Award. He has exhibited his work at the Art Institute of Chicago, the Cedar Rapids Museum of Art, the Detroit Institute of Art, the Cleveland Museum of Art, the School of Visual Arts, and the Society of Illustrators. He is a graduate of the University of the Arts in Philadelphia, Pennsylvania, and holds a master's degree in illustration from the School of Visual Arts in New York City. He lives in Brooklyn, New York, with his wife, Andrea, with whom he often collaborates, and his two children. Visit him online at www.brianpinkney.net. ("Jabari Unmasked," p. 37.)

SEAN G. QUALLS is an award-winning Brooklyn-based artist who is a children's book illustrator and author. He has illustrated a number of highly acclaimed books for children, including *Giant Steps to Change the World* by Spike Lee and Tonya Lewis Lee; *Little Cloud and Lady Wind* by Toni Morrison and her son Slade; and *Before John Was a Jazz Giant* by Carole Boston Weatherford, for which he received a Coretta Scott King Illustration Honor award. His work has received two Blue Ribbon citations from the Bulletin of the Center for Children's Books, where he was also cited for his "serious craftsmanship" and "original style." Qualls has created illustrations for magazines, newspapers, and advertisements. His work has been shown in galleries in New York and across the country. Some of his most recent titles include *Emmanuel's Dream* (a Schneider Family Book Award winner) written by Laurie Ann Thompson as well as *The Case for Loving* and *Two Friends*, both of which he illustrated with his wife, illustrator/author Selina Alko. He lives in Brooklyn, New York, (where you can find him DJing on occasion) with his wife and their two children. Visit him online at www.seanqualls.com. ("Common Denominator," p. 93.)

JAMES E. RANSOME has been illustrating children's books for over twenty-five years with almost sixty picture books, many book jackets, greeting cards, and magazines to his name. Winner of several awards for his illustrations, including Coretta Scott King awards and an NAACP Image Award, Mr. Ransome received his BFA in illustration from Pratt Institute in New York. The MTA Metro-North Railroad selected him to illustrate one in a series of posters for the New York City subway system. Ransome's work is part of both private and public children's book art collections and a number of commissioned murals, including three for the Underground Railroad Museum in Cincinnati, Ohio. He lives in Rhinebeck, New York, with his wife, author Lesa Cline-Ransome, and their four children. Visit him online at www.jamesransome .com. ("Emergency Measures," p. 13 and "I Leave the Glory Days," p. 95.)

JAVAKA STEPTOE is an eclectic artist and illustrator whose debut work, *In Daddy's Arms I Am Tall: African Americans Celebrating Fathers*, earned him the Coretta Scott King Illustrator Award, a nomination for Outstanding Children's Literary Work at the NAACP Image Awards, a finalist ranking for the Texas Bluebonnet Award, and many other honors. His books *Do You Know What I'll Do?* written by Charlotte Zolotow and *A Pocketful of Poems* written by Nikki Grimes received starred reviews from both *Publishers Weekly* and *Booklist*. *Hot Day on Abbott Avenue* written by Karen English received a 2005 Jane Addams Children's Book Award Honor. Steptoe is also the author/illustrator of *The Jones Family Express*, and he illustrated *Rain Play* by Cynthia Cotten and *Amiri and Odette: A Love Story* by multi-award-winning author Walter Dean Myers. Once a model and inspiration for his late father, award-winning author/illustrator John Steptoe, Javaka Steptoe has established himself as an outstanding illustrator in his own right. Visit him online at www.javaka.com. ("In Search of a Superpower," p. 55.)

SHADRA STRICKLAND studied design, writing, and illustration at Syracuse University and later went on to complete her MFA at the School of Visual Arts in New York City. She is an award-winning illustrator and a professor of illustration at the Maryland Institute College of Art in Baltimore, Maryland. The illustration for "No Hamsters Here" was created using the linocut reduction printmaking technique. It was inspired by the work of Harlem Renaissance artist James Lesesne Wells. Visit her online at www.jumpin.shadrastrickland.com. ("No Hamsters Here," p. 49.)

ELIZABETH ZUNON was born in Albany, New York, and spent her childhood in the Ivory Coast (Côte d'Ivoire), West Africa. Surrounded by the bright, vibrant colors of everyday West African fabrics and tropical vegetation, Ms. Zunon's love of color and pattern grew, lingered, and is a fixture today in all of her works. After returning to the United States, she attended the Rhode Island School of Design and graduated with a BFA in illustration. Ms. Zunon now lives in Albany, where she explores a multicultural world through painting, beading, sewing, and collage. Her picture book *The Boy Who Harnessed the Wind* was chosen for the Cooperative Children's Book Center's 2013 Best-of-the-year list. Visit her online at www.lizzunon.com. ("Crucible of Champions," p. 23.)

ACKNOWLEDGMENTS

I will be forever grateful to Victoria Wells Arms, who was crazy enough to say yes to a project unlike anything she'd ever seen.

Thanks to Brett Wright, who enthusiastically jumped on board with both feet.

Thanks to Amy Malskeit, who read an early draft of this work with a keen eye, and offered sound suggestions for improvement.

Thanks to agent Elizabeth Harding, my chief cheerleader, who took on the mammoth task of acquiring permissions.

Thanks to artist Nancy Gary Ward, who gave me tips on ideation as I contemplated my first illustration. Thanks, also, to illustrator Lea Lyon, who critiqued my early sketches and gave valuable feedback.

Finally, thanks to my art group, Montage, for always encouraging me to explore new avenues of creativity, especially when it means walking into my fear.

What a fabulous team I have around me!

SOURCES

POEMS

Gwendolyn Bennett: "To Usward" (page 51) and "To a Dark Girl" (page 70) © Gwendolyn Bennett Papers. Sc MG 77. Manuscripts, Archives and Rare Books Division. Schomburg Center for Research in Black Culture, New York Public Library.

Countee Cullen: "For a Poet" (page 25) © Countee Cullen, Amistad Research Center.

Waring Cuney: "No Images" (page 85) from *Beltway: A Poetry Quarterly*, washingtonart.com/beltway/cuney/html.

Paul Laurence Dunbar: "We Wear the Mask" (page 34) from *Lyrics of Lowly Life*, 1896.

Langston Hughes: "Mother to Son" (page 38) and "The Negro Speaks of Rivers" (page 65) from THE COLLECTED POEMS OF LANGSTON HUGHES by Langston Hughes, edited by Arnold Rampersad with David Roessel, Associate Editor, copyright © 1994 by the Estate of Langston Hughes. Used by permission of Alfred A. Knopf, an imprint of the Knopf Doubleday Publishing Group, a division of Penguin Random House LLC. All rights reserved.

Georgia Douglas Johnson: "Calling Dreams" (page 31), "Hope" (page 56), and "Common Dust" (page 77) from *Selected Works of Georgia Douglas Johnson*, G.K. Hall & Co., an imprint of Simon & Schuster, 1997.

Clara Ann Thompson: "Life and Death" (page 18) and "The Minor Key" (page 90) © Clara Ann Thompson, *Voices in the Poetic Tradition*, G.K. Hall & Co., an imprint of Simon & Schuster, 1996.

Jean Toomer: "Storm Ending" (page 15) and "As the Eagle Soars" (page 47) Courtesy of the Yale Collection of American Literature, Yale University.

POET PORTRAITS

Gwendolyn Bennett (page 99): Schomburg Center for Research in Black Culture, Photographs and Prints Division, New York Public Library, 1924.

Countee Cullen (page 100): © Library of Congress, Prints & Photographs Division, Carl Van Vechten Collection, LC-USZ62-42529.

Waring Cuney (page 100): the African American Registry, http://www.aaregistry.org/historic_events/view/waring-cuney-poet-harlem-rennissance.

Paul Laurence Dunbar (page 101): Schomburg Center for Research in Black Culture, New York Library.

Langston Hughes (page 102): © Library of Congress, Prints & Photographs Division, Carl Van Vechten Collection, LC-USZ62-92598.

Georgia Douglas Johnson (page 103): Schomburg Center for Research in Black Culture, New York Library.

Clara Ann Thompson (page 104): *Songs from the Wayside,* Clara Ann Thompson, 1908, http://archive.org/stream/songsfromwayside00thom#page/n7/mode/2up.

Jean Toomer (page 105): Wiki Spaces, Harlem Renaissance Poets, http://harlemrenaissancepoets.wikispaces.com/Jean+Toomer+-+Miranda+Jessop.

INDEX

Note: *Italic* page numbers indicate illustrations.